MURDER
ON
MARAWA PRIME

Vonnie Winslow Crist

Pole to Pole Publishing

Pole to Pole Publishing
Baltimore

Books by Vonnie Winslow Crist:

Story Collections
Owl Light
The Greener Forest

Novel
The Enchanted Skean

Novelette
Murder on Marawa Prime

Children's Book
Leprechaun Cake & Other Tales

Poetry Collections
River of Stars
Essential Fables

Murder on Marawa Prime

Published 2016 by Pole to Pole Publishing
Book and Cover Design Copyright © 2016 Pole to Pole Publishing
www.poletopolepublishing.com
Cover art copyright © breaker213 /CanStockPhoto

ISBN-10: 1-941559-09-3
ISBN-13: 978-1-941559-09-3

Library of Congress Control Number: 2016940249

Acknowledgements

Thanks to my writing friends for their support—most especially Kelly A. Harmon, Katie Hartlove, Patti Kinlock, and Wendy Stevens. Thank you to Pole to Pole Publishing for taking a chance on Murder on Marawa Prime. And as ever, thanks to my family and friends for supporting my creative endeavors–even if they have no interest whatsoever in speculative fiction. Lastly, a special thank you to Ernie for always being there.

Ernie, this one is for you.

MURDER
ON
MARAWA PRIME

*F*lynn was wearing dead man's shoes, or to be more exact, sitting in a dead man's seat. After driver Spider Varley had been found garroted, but before he'd been cremated, Brownstone Management reassigned his bus route to Flynn. A promotion of sorts, available only because of Spider's murder.

The Gulzar to Antiquity City Loop was the most desirable bus route in this sector. Well-to-do tourists interested in archaeological finds, ancient ruins, and mineral springs water complexes boarded climate-controlled vehicles at the capital city's main transport station. With nothing to do but sit back and enjoy the scenery, the wealthy relaxed while their tour-guide/driver shuttled them from one site to another. And as a bonus, the route offered passengers eager to try their hand at games of chance, a convenient transfer station for a side trip to The Canyons gambling mecca.

Brownstone advertised and delivered a luxury experience to its customers. With his distinguished gray mustache and university-educated bearing, Spider had embodied everything Brownstone stood for. Unfortunately for him, somebody wanted his lucrative route, and was willing to commit murder to acquire it.

And that's what worried Flynn. His past dealings with Marawa Prime law enforcers included misunderstandings and small infractions—killing wasn't in his nature. But it was in someone's nature, and Flynn was assigned the route they coveted. He'd have to keep his eyes open until he returned to Gulzar and requested a transfer to a less dangerous position.

With Spider's untimely demise still on his mind, Flynn shifted in his seat, scanned the horizon for distinctive landmarks, and wished Brownstone had given this route to anyone but him.

*A*s the hill country of Marawa Prime gave way to the mountains, Flynn finally spotted kilometer marker 247. He punched in the speaker code and began his tour-guide talk.

"If you look out the windows on the left side of the bus, you will see the second tallest peak on Marawa Prime. The Earther, Takoda Wilchester, mapped this area in the second century after the great Walloong Moon Quakes. This particular peak is named Starleen's Bosom, in honor of Takoda's long-suffering wife."

Flynn paused. As he waited for the view of the mountain and its name to sink in, he tucked a strand of his shoulder-length hair behind his ear. The responses of the passengers were as predictable as nightfall. While the women squealed, then giggled; the men on the vehicle smirked.

With his left hand, Flynn adjusted the rear view mirror. His shirt sleeve was pushed up, so the dragon tattoo which wound its way around his forearm was clearly visible. The tattoo marked him as a Traveler, but he doubted anyone on the bus understood the significance of his body art. Still, if a killer were on board, perhaps he or she would think twice before wrapping a wire around Flynn's neck. Travelers believed in revenge. Kill one, and others would pursue you until the blood debt was paid.

After surveying the road in front of him, Flynn glanced in the mirror again and studied the people. He shook his head. With the thrill of seeing Starleen's Bosom passed, they were talking with each other, ignoring the splendid rock formations jutting up on either side of the highway. The only person bothering to observe the Marawa scenery was a pale woman two rows back in seat 2A-Left. Hunched low with a rat-tailed pet draped around her shoulders, she gazed out the window as the setting sun tinted the rockscape shades of crimson, orange, and maroon.

Flynn activated the speaker again. "We will be stopping in about fifteen minutes at The Wayfarer for refreshments and a night's rest. For those interested in visiting The Canyons, information is available at the check-in counter."

The chattering passengers barely acknowledged his announcement. He sighed, tapped in the silence code, then heard the unpleasant trilling of a singing opossum. The noisy creature seemed to take great pleasure in warbling off-key. If the marsupial hadn't belonged to the woman in 2A-Left, Flynn would probably have ordered the passenger to silence the opossum or get it off of the bus. But when he had glanced at the woman a few minutes ago, she'd appeared rather forlorn, so he resolved to ignore the noise until the bus stopped at The Wayfarer.

He looked in his mirror again. The marsupial was scrutinizing him, its jewel eyes glittering like peridots. After giving Flynn a toothy grin, it trilled, and nuzzled its owner. As he watched, the young woman stroked the opossum's fur and whispered into the marsupial's ear. The tenderness on the girl's face when she touched her pet caused Flynn to clear his throat.

Perhaps, she had heard him, because the girl suddenly looked up into his gaze. Flynn shifted his focus to the highway, but not before noticing her eyes didn't match. Her left iris was bright green and her right iris was dove gray. He wondered what her name was. Something mysterious, he expected.

Flynn pulled into The Wayfarer's parking garage, stopped the bus, climbed out, unlocked the storage compartments on either side of the solar vehicle, and began to unload the suitcases, knapsacks, duffel bags, and other traveling gear. He was finished unloading the storage compartments before more than a handful of people got off of the bus. So while Flynn waited for the remaining passengers to exit, he leaned against a support column with one leather-booted foot crossed in front of the other. He casually smiled, nodded at the tourists, and looked for a killer among them.

One by one, the passengers filed out of the bus. After each person exited the vehicle, they pointed to their belongings and a uniformed bell hop grabbed their luggage. Used to others handling all manual labor, the wealthy paid little attention to those who served them. Instead, they chatted among themselves and strolled into the complex.

Flynn hoped many of them would leave an electronic tip for him when they checked-in at the traveling facility. If he'd been charming enough since departing Gulzar, the tips would cover his room, dinner, and breakfast with plenty of credits to spare.

He straightened up as the last person stepped off of the bus.

"Sorry about, Hoshi," said the young woman with the mismatched eyes as she stepped towards him.

He noted the opossum's tail was wrapped around her neck as it rode upon her shoulder. "No problem," Flynn lied. "As long as other passengers don't complain."

"Sorry, just the same." The woman actually picked up her luggage, turned, and began to walk towards The Wayfarer's check-in area.

"Hey, um, Miss. Got plans for dinner?" Flynn sounded awkward, even to himself.

"No." The girl laughed.

Flynn thought of wind chimes.

"Flynn," he said as he stepped forward and stuck out his right hand.

"Natsu." The girl set down her duffel bag and slipped her small hand into his.

He noticed her skin was warm—almost hot. The opossum inspected Flynn from its perch on Natsu's left shoulder. It hummed softly.

"I have to eat in the atrium, so Hoshi can stay with me. If that's not a problem, it would be fun to have company."

He noticed after she finished speaking, her lips remained slightly parted. Almost as if she wanted to say something else.

"That would be great. I love opossums." Flynn hoped he sounded sincere. The marsupial blinked twice at him, then increased its humming.

The girl's lips curled into a smile. "Seven o'clock, then?"

"Yeah. Sounds perfect. I'll be there, down near the fountain and fish pool."

Natsu nodded agreement, then turned, and walked to the check-in desk.

Flynn stumbled as he climbed back into the bus. After parking the vehicle in the designated area, he jogged to his room. He showered, dropping the soap several times. Then, he had trouble buttoning his clean shirt and nearly forgot his room key when he hurried out the door to dinner. Arriving at the atrium first, Flynn had time to notice the calla lilies blooming near the fish pool were the same ivory as Natsu's skin.

"Punctual. I like that in a man," said a musical voice behind him.

Flynn stood. His belt buckle caught on the edge of the café table, tilting it enough to upset the two tumblers of water he had ordered from the waitress. With a quick grab, he managed to save one tumbler, but the other tumbler, water, ice cubes, and silverware bounced, splashed, and skittled across the floor tiles.

"Oh, sh…" he caught himself. "Oh, shoot."

"Don't worry about it." Natsu touched the back of his hand. "We all make mistakes."

His skin tingled. *Get a grip*, he thought. *You're falling too fast for some girl you don't know.*

"We can sit over there, closer to the waterfall," suggested the girl as she pointed to a table nearer to the pool's edge.

"Sure." Flynn followed the woman and her opossum. As she walked, he contemplated Natsu's long hair as it swished back and forth, mimicking the movement of her hips. Hoshi peeked over Natsu's shoulder at him. Flynn had the uncomfortable feeling the marsupial knew what he was thinking.

Once they were seated at a table so close to the waterfall Flynn felt a light mist dampening his arm, they ordered drinks and dinner.

"Tell me about yourself," Natsu said as she sipped a fruit drink. The beverage came with a little pink umbrella and a tropical flower blossom which the girl was twirling with her fingers. He liked the fact her fingernails were not painted, but natural.

"Not much to tell." Flynn swirled the last inch of beer in his glass and stared into the girl's odd eyes. "I left home in my teens. Wanderlust, I guess. Worked a dozen jobs in a dozen different cities. Wait a minute." He thought about his answer. "Truth be told, I probably worked two dozen or more jobs in two dozen cities. And now, driving a cross-country bus gives me a chance to see more of Marawa Prime and meet lots of people. I'll probably do it a while longer—unless something better turns up." *Or until someone kills me for Spider's route,* he silently added.

Natsu nodded, but seemed uncertain whether to speak.

Flynn liked the way she rested her chin on her hand when she listened to him talk. *Slow down, lover boy,* he told himself. *This isn't like you to leap before you look.*

"How about you?"

"Hoshi and I left Gulzar in a bit of a rush." She stroked the opossum before continuing, "I would like to visit some of the ancient ruins near here. Maybe find a quiet town to settle in."

Her pet warbled, and then, winked at Flynn.

"Gulzar? So you come from the coast. Were you a student at the university?"

"No," Natsu bit her lip and leaned closer to Flynn. "I was at the Ziya Research Facility."

"Are you a scientist, then?"

"No," Natsu hushed her voice to a whisper. "I am one of the experiments. I was genetically bred to work in a dim laboratory on projects that demand low light, but my aptitudes didn't fit within the parameters of the position."

"So you weren't scientist material then?"

Natsu shook her head. "It is not that I don't excel at science, I am just not able to see well enough in dim light for their needs." She stroked the gray opossum, who now sprawled on the café table, and continued, "Hoshi is a reject, too. She wouldn't learn the tunes requested by the buyers, so she was left in the breeding kennels to die."

"That's cruel. Of course, it *is* a government facility. The government administrators rarely consider how their decisions impact us regular folk."

"I agree. Which is why," she leaned even closer to Flynn before adding, "I stole her."

He choked on his beer as their waitress set dinner on the table. Immediately, the opossum crouched over her plate of farm-raised trout and gulped the glistening flesh.

"Are the officials searching for you?" Flynn surveyed the atrium looking for law enforcers and/or Spider's killer. But it was impossible to zero in on someone out of place, since the room was now bustling with waitresses, busboys, servants, and tourists and their pets.

"I don't know. I don't think so." Natsu kept her eyes focused on her plate; poked the stir-fry with her fork.

"So the opossum is genetically engineered and stolen?"

"Yes," answered Natsu as she lifted her eyes to meet Flynn's gaze. Her lower lip quivered. "Even products of the arti-wombs deserve choices. Deserve a life."

"I understand. I mean, I'm all for equality for Gen-Engs—but not everyone's comfortable around…"

"Freaks."

"That's not what I was going to say."

"But you were thinking it." Tears were about to spill down Natsu's cheeks when the opossum wailed and leaped into the girl's arms.

A flash of orange fabric drew Flynn's attention to a blond-haired woman behind Natsu. The woman pulled a dart blower from her sleeve, then lifted the weapon to her lips. He grabbed Natsu's tropical drink and hurled the glass at the assassin. The missile knocked the wooden tube out of the killer's hands.

"Come on," he said, pulling the girl and her pet out of the atrium and through the crowded lobby. "There's no telling if that dart was meant for you, the opossum, or me."

"Okay," said Natsu as he continued to hold her hand.

"This way." Flynn dragged the girl, with her pet still clinging to her, into a service elevator, through the service hallways, and to his room. He shoved the pair inside, then locked the door behind them and turned to Natsu. "It seems someone *is* interested in you and the opossum. Or," he rubbed his hands together trying to erase Natsu's warmth from his flesh, "they could be after me for the bus route."

"The bus route?"

"Long story," he responded. "Let's just say where credits are involved, killing is a choice some people are willing to make."

"I don't want to meet those people." Natsu frowned, then continued, "But I believe the assassin was after Hoshi and me. You see, we wouldn't be the first Ziya experiment failures to be murdered."

"What?"

"I'm sorry. I don't want you involved. We'll go to our room, get our stuff, and find another ride across Marawa."

"You can't go back to your room. And anything leaving the traveling complex now is sure to be watched, no matter who the assassin is after." Flynn pressed his fingertips to his forehead. He had been in tougher spots before. He just needed to get a plan in place.

"What room were you in?"

"Thirteen-forty-seven. It's on the first floor on the other side of the atrium."

"Give me the key."

"If I can't go back there, you shouldn't either."

"I shouldn't, but a member of the cleaning staff pushing a cart or a trash-collecting bin could. Stay here. Don't open the door for anyone. I'll be back soon and," Flynn added with a sigh, "do *not* let the opossum start singing."

Natsu nodded and sat down on his bed with the soft-furred marsupial curled in her lap.

A *few credits in the right account, and a woman from* housekeeping retrieved Natsu's gear for Flynn. Within an hour, he was back in his room with the girl's knapsack and duffel bag.

"I was afraid you would bring security," Natsu said.

"I'm in this too far." He lifted his hands, and then, let them drop to either side of his body. "Law enforcers probably wouldn't believe a plea of innocence from me anyway. I've been involved in a few fly-by-night deals in the past."

Natsu's eyes widened.

"Nothing serious. Mostly, I was a bystander when a cousin of mine decided to do something shady."

"I see."

But he knew she didn't see. She'd never met his cousin or been a part of a blood clan. You just didn't turn on a fellow Traveler. You accepted his punishment as yours if necessary.

Flynn sat on the bed beside Natsu. This close to her, he could barely breathe. *Stay focused*, he reminded himself before speaking.

"We need to sleep for a couple of hours, then leave tomorrow morning before sunrise."

"What about your job?" She placed her hand on his thigh.

He felt her warmth through the denim.

"About time to move on." Flynn thought of Spider's death and added, "to be honest, no job is worth a knife in the back." He winked and continued, "But let's look at the bright side of things, I think something better might have just come along."

Ready to sleep on the floor if he'd misread her feelings, Flynn drew Natsu towards him. Begrudgingly, the opossum jumped from her shoulder onto the headboard.

"I agree," she replied with a smile as she tilted her head and slid her arms around his neck.

*F*lynn observed Natsu as she slept. Her skin glowed like the moon on a hazy night. His arm wrapped around her was a dark shadow obscuring some of her radiance. He propped himself up on one elbow, traced the outline of a heart on her belly with his forefinger, then leaned over Natsu's face, drawn to her warmth and light. The opossum lifted its head, glared at him with iridescent green eyes, and then, growled—showing all fifty of its pointy teeth.

"Hoshi? What's wrong?" Natsu's eyelids open; she struggled to sit up.

"Ssh." Flynn silenced them both. "It's time to get started, and we don't want to draw attention to ourselves."

The girl nodded, slipped her sweater and jeans back on. Hoshi kneaded the pillow on which Natsu's head had been resting with her front paws and glowered at Flynn.

"We've got to consolidate our gear," he explained. "A knapsack a piece and one duffel bag between us. Besides," he pointed at the opossum, "you need to keep your arms free to carry Hoshi."

"Absolutely," she answered, and emptied some of the things from her duffel bag.

After she was done, Flynn stuffed as much of his gear as possible into the bag. Flynn picked up Natsu's knapsack, helped her slide her arms into the straps, then struggled to buckle on his overloaded backpack. It was a good thing his last job before bus driver had involved heavy-lifting. He'd added a lot of muscle and managed to retain it by hauling suitcases in and out of the storage area under the bus.

"We're leaving through the loading docks. The delivery trucks started arriving about two hours ago. Some of them should be pulling out and heading to the next tourist station any time now."

Flynn stuck his head out the door, checked for people, then signaled Natsu to follow him as he stepped into the hall. "I know a few of the truckers. Believe me, most don't mind duping the security forces every now and then."

When Flynn, Natsu, and the opossum reached the loading docks, about a dozen trucks were close to departure. And when one of the drivers turned around, he knew they had a way out of their predicament.

"Hey, Jaffee," Flynn called to a burly man with longish hair. "Got room for a couple of stowaways?"

"If you have credits to treat me to lunch down the road apiece, I got the room." The teamster studied the couple for a moment, then raised his eyebrows. "I didn't know you was attached, Flynn."

"Yeah," said Flynn. "This is my partner, Natsu, and our opossum, Hoshi." Flynn couldn't believe how easy it was to say *partner* after only knowing the girl a day.

"Nice to meet you, sir," said Natsu.

Flynn noticed she didn't offer her hand to Jaffee, instead shyly nodding. As he would expect, the opossum showed its teeth and growled at the truck driver.

Jaffee tapped the brim of his hat with the first two fingers of his left hand. "The pleasure is mine." The trucker clapped Flynn on the back. "Climb in, buddy. I gotta hear how you got yourself hooked up with these two."

For the first hour of the trip, Jaffee entertained Flynn and Natsu with exaggerated tales of a trucker's life. "Ain't nothing I won't haul if the price is right," he bragged, then chuckled. "And now that we are two hundred kilometers down the road, tell me what's really going on here."

"You can still claim ignorance," warned Flynn.

"I may be ignorant, but I know a load of bull when it's slung at me. What's going on?"

"I am a flawed experiment from the Ziya Research Facility in Gulzar. So is Hoshi. We ran away, and we don't want to ever go back. We met Flynn, and..."

"We hit it off," finished Flynn.

The trucker pursed his lips, leaned forward, and peered around Flynn at the girl. "What were they doing to you?"

Jaffee refocused on the roadway, his pleasant expression changing to a scowl as Natsu talked.

"The Ziya staff decided to breed a group of arti-womb humans who could work in near darkness. Some biological and chemical research has to be done in limited light, you know."

"So what, you can see in the dark?" the trucker asked.

"I can't," answered Natsu, "but Hoshi can. I can see with my gray eye in dusky light, but I can't see in total darkness. Which is unacceptable."

"Explains the weird eyes." Jaffee glanced at the girl, then added, "Sorry about the weird comment."

"It's okay. I have been called worse."

"Tell him the rest," urged Flynn.

He wanted Jaffee on their side. Jaffee and Flynn had always been a good team in a scrape. If the girl and her pet were the targets, he knew it wouldn't take the assassin long to figure out whose truck they'd climbed into and where they were headed.

"In the experiment I was a part of, the Ziya scientists inserted fluorescent genes from jellyfish, sea anemones, and algae into fertilized human eggs. They used their own gametes, so the zygotes that they altered were supposed to be super-smart babies. And most of us were gifted, though not always in science as our parents had hoped."

"How many of you are there?"

Good, thought Flynn. *Jaffee is touched by her plight.* Flynn knew you could always count on blood.

"There were ninety-six zygotes, but only fifty-three of us made it out of the arti-wombs. Of the fifty-three that were born, twenty-five died within two years of one genetic problem or the other. The twenty-eight who remained all exhibited glowing skin and had at least one dim-vision eye. The problem was, their gifts varied. After years of intense training, it was determined only thirteen of the super-babies were gifted in science and therefore suitable for the original breeding purpose. Of those, only seven had dim-vision ability in both eyes."

"Seven out of ninety-six and millions of tax-payer's credits used. Poor success rate, I'd say. Now, someone needs to take the blame," added Flynn.

The teamster grunted. "Which is why they canceled the program. But why are they after you?" Jaffee scratched his chin, then gave a quick look in Natsu's direction.

The girl sighed. The opossum began a low hum. "I don't think failure was an option. The fifteen luminescent Gen-Engs not super-scientist material, were released from the program first. One by one, they disappeared or had unfortunate accidents. Next, the six Gen-Engs with dim-vision ability in only one eye were released. They, too, began to vanish." Natsu ran her fingers down either side of Hoshi's backbone before continuing, "I think I might be the last one left alive."

"Safest solution is to erase the failed part of the project," said Flynn. "And we both know how easy it is to get away with murder on Marawa."

Jaffee grunted. "How many assassins? And how many hours are they behind us?"

"We don't know how many," answered Flynn. He decided not to mention Spider's garroting or the possibility he might be a target, too. Truth be told, the minute Flynn didn't show up for work this morning, Brownstone would assign someone else the Gulzar to Antiquity City Loop.

"I discouraged one woman at The Wayfarer. She had a blowpipe. I assume she was using a toxin that mimics heart failure, epileptic fit, or a similar medical problem. If she's determined to off Natsu, she's probably an hour or two behind us." Flynn shrugged his shoulders. "Maybe even three hours behind. Funny thing is, I remember her from the bus—she transferred on yesterday morning."

The opossum began to trill.

"Opossum is Gen-Eng, too. Right?" observed the trucker.

"Yes," said Natsu. "Even though she isn't what her breeders wanted, Hoshi has a prehensile tail, razor-sharp teeth, and she can see in total darkness."

The trucker snorted. "I bet she's a helluva guard beast."

"She is." The girl stroked the marsupial and quieted her singing. "We really appreciate the ride, Jaffee, and I apologize for involving you in this."

"Apologize?" Jaffee laughed. "My life has been boring since the last time Flynn asked me for a favor. I count on meeting this troublemaker every now and again. Keeps me on my toes."

For all his bravado, Flynn noticed sweat trickling down Jaffee's forehead and dripping from his chin.

"I've got a plan," said Flynn.

"You've always got a plan," said the truck driver as he adjusted his side mirrors. "What's it gonna cost me?"

"Nothing. You just need to keep driving, and I'll give Momma a call."

"She's gonna want you to stay this time." Jaffee wiped his brow with the back of his sleeve.

Flynn looked down at Natsu. She was pressed against him, her hand clutching his. He glanced behind the seat. The opossum was stretched out in the berth, napping on top of their packs. "I plan to settle in The Canyons and work in one of Momma's places."

Jaffee shook his head and pointed at the communication panel. "You'd better call in and get the ball rolling."

Flynn punched in a series of numbers. There was some static; then, a woman answered. "Momma Tereza, owner of The Third Eye, can I help you?"

"Momma, it's Flynn. I'm bringing someone home for you to meet. We want to settle in The Canyons, but we're in a bit of a jam."

The cab of the truck was silent—even Hoshi stared at the panel and waited for a response.

Flynn recalled all the times he'd sworn to Momma he would stay in The Canyons and help her run The Third Eye. He had worked the craps tables, card tables, roulette wheels, bars, restaurants—even the kitchens at one time or the other. But he'd never really had a girl worth keeping before or worth settling down with; now, he had one he couldn't face losing.

What goes around, comes around, he thought as he rubbed the stubble on his chin. He had always been a heart breaker, never committing to any woman, much less believing in love at first sight.

"You got me, karma," he muttered under his breath before saying out loud, "Momma, are you still there?"

"How soon are you arriving?" Momma Tereza's voice was thick. Flynn could tell she was crying.

"Maybe an hour, maybe less."

"Barreling in like a herd of cattle, I'm sure," said Momma.

Flynn nudged Jaffee with his elbow.

"I guess you'll be ready for a shower and change of clothes?" the owner of The Third Eye continued.

"Yes. Make that two showers!"

Momma's throaty laughter blasted from the communication panel. "See you soon, Flynn." The speaker went quiet.

"Kitchen entrance, livestock ramp is where we're to pull up. And you're to go directly to her compartments," said Jaffee.

"I know. Haven't forgotten everything, cousin."

Natsu leaned forward, examined the faces of the two men. "You're cousins?"

"Yes. If you're from The Canyons, odds are you're related," said Flynn. "Centuries ago when Marawa Prime was settled, some of the workers…"

"He means the grunts," added Jaffee.

"As I was saying," continued Flynn. "Some of the workers bought land in the middle of what was then a wilderness area and built a city."

"Gamblers' Dream, Thieves' Paradise, Travelers' City."

"Jaffee, let me finish." Flynn took his hand, tilted Natsu's chin up so he could see her eyes. "The workers were Travelers, Gypsies. And that's what we are—Jaffee and me and Momma. That's what most of the residents of The Canyons are. Once I take you to Momma Tereza, once we break laws for you, you become one of us. There is no going back to Gulzar, or anywhere else for that matter, unless Momma sends you."

"We want to stay with you, Flynn," the girl said. "There is nothing for us back in Gulzar and," Natsu leaned closer. "And you're here."

The opossum crept back into her lap. Ignoring the humans, it groomed its back leg.

"You gotta lose the name, Natsu," said Jaffee. Lips pressed tightly together, he seemed focused on the road ahead.

"The scientists at Ziya gave it to me because I was born in the summer. Eleven other girls had the same name. It would be nice to have a name picked just for me."

"How about Nadia?" Flynn kissed her brow. "Nadia means hope."

The girl nodded. "What about Hoshi? Do we need to change her name, too?"

"Hell, yes! Oh, sh…" Jaffee slammed the steering wheel with his hand. "Sorry, not used to lady passengers. You gotta change the opossum's name, too. People will remember a singing opossum named Hoshi."

"How about Honey?" the girl asked as she caressed the marsupial's neck. "She is sweet like honey, and it sounds close enough to Hoshi, so she should know I'm talking to her." The opossum tipped its head, pushed against Nadia's scratching fingers.

"Nadia and her singing opossum, Honey. It sounds like a new attraction at The Third Eye already!" chuckled Jaffee.

Flynn glared at his cousin, but didn't comment.

Half an hour later, as their truck sped the last few kilometers to their destination, Nadia gasped as the city seemed to spring from the rocks. "I can see why it's called The Canyons. How long did it take to build?"

"Centuries," answered Flynn. "The Travelers carved the first buildings into the natural canyons, then built a stone and steel city out from there. Now, it's the gaming capitol of Marawa Prime."

"How many people live here?"

"Thousands more than the authorities know about," bragged Jaffee. "And most are involved in more than gaming."

Flynn nudged his cousin again.

"Maybe half a million residents," said Flynn. "Of course, if you count the gamers, vacationers, and other passers-through… two or three million during the warm months. Maybe a million to a million and a half in the off-season."

"I suppose a lot of people come here from Gulzar and the other coastal cities?"

"Not to worry," said Flynn. "No one will find you here."

Natsu-now-Nadia smiled and squeezed his hand.

* * *

*T**he traffic picked up as they drove closer to the center** of the rock and metal city. There were buses, trucks, and all-terrains wending their way from the airport, train depot, and helipad. On either side of the highway, homes and businesses jostled one another for space. Eventually, The Canyons loomed above the truck and its passengers like a forest of mammoth trees above an ant.

Suddenly, Jaffee flipped on his turn signal and drove into an underground maze of tunnels lit by rows and rows of cup-lights embedded in the tiling.

"How do you know where to turn?" Nadia inquired. Her pet was now perched on the dashboard, peering through the windshield into the tunnel ahead.

"Signs," said Flynn as he pointed to an overhead panel that announced: The Third Eye–Exit 13.

"Memory," said Jaffee as he tapped his head. "Some of us have stayed close to home, learned The Canyons' tunnels and passages like a Butte Tiger learns its territory."

"Ouch!" Flynn slapped his hand on his chest and grinned.

"Just calling it like I see it, Cuz."

"You're lucky, Jaffee—you always knew what you wanted. I had to wander most of Marawa Prime to realize where I belong." He gazed down at Nadia. "And who I belonged with."

Nadia smiled and looked up at Flynn. "What if your mother doesn't like me? What if she hates opossums?"

Flynn caressed her cheek, then drew his forefinger along her jawbone. "She will like you, and believe me, she'll love the opossum." Honey closed her eyes and began to warble as Flynn kissed Nadia.

"Yeoh, come up for air. We're here." Jaffee pulled his rig up to the livestock unloading area. Flynn struggled with their gear while Nadia climbed down from the cab with Honey clinging to her.

"Let me give you a hand with that stuff," offered Jaffee. "I think Momma is gonna want to see you pronto."

Before Flynn could answer, a corrugated metal door rolled up. There, in the steel door frame, stood a woman of enormous proportions. Her flaming red hair was bedecked with gems and charms.

The woman stepped forward and threw her arms around Flynn. "Finally, you have come home to Momma."

After another hug and several kisses on each cheek, Flynn cleared his throat. "Momma, this is Natsu, now called Nadia, and her opossum, Hoshi, now called Honey."

The huge woman inspected the girl and her pet, and then, studied her son's eyes. Flynn knew it was obvious he had fallen head over heels for Natsu-now-Nadia.

"Welcome, Nadia. I have always wanted a daughter," Momma Tereza announced and hugged the startled girl. The agile opossum scooted around to the back of Nadia's shoulders, and then, jumped into Flynn's arms to avoid being crushed.

His mother raised her tattooed eyebrows. "I never thought you cared much for marsupials, Flynn. This Honey must be special."

"She is," answered Flynn as the opossum hummed.

"Momma, you need to get them inside, and I've got to move the truck," said Jaffee. "There's at least one assassin following us, and there could be more."

Momma Tereza patted Jaffee on his cheek. "Good boy. Park the truck in the casino warehouse and meet us up in my rooms." As Jaffee departed, Momma wrapped an arm around Nadia and led the girl into the bowels of The Third Eye. Flynn followed, still carrying the opossum.

*W*alking *a couple of steps behind the women, Flynn* noted how different they were. And yet, his mother had embraced this wisp of a girl he'd brought home. Natsu-now-Nadia, seemed relaxed and was listening intently to his mother's guided tour of the casino. Flynn had neither seen or heard the baggage boy, who had by now taken their gear to the family area of the complex. He smiled. His mother still ran an effective organization.

"And this," he heard Momma say, "is where our clients come to have their fortunes told."

Below them stretched a sea of gaudy tents. In each tent, there was a future speaker or spiritual adviser of some kind, and one or more clients eager to pay a few credits for advice or insight.

"I could work here," said Nadia.

Momma's eyes narrowed. "What do you mean?"

"I can read tea leaves. Well, not really read them—they don't spell anything out. But when the Gen-Engs and employees at the Ziya Research Facility drank a cup of tea, I would have them turn the cup around in their hands three times, and then, invert it on a saucer. When I flipped the cup back over, I could see animals and symbols in the leaves."

"Did someone teach you to do this?"

"No," said Nadia shaking her head. "The animals and symbols seemed to tell a story when I studied them. I would tell my friends the stories that came to my mind." The girl lowered her eyes. "I'm sorry, I didn't mean to upset you. It was just a game like a lot of other games I played to keep from being bored."

Momma Tereza looked over the girl's head at Flynn.

"It's the first I've heard of it," he said.

"What other games did you play?" Momma's brow was furrowed as she continued, "Don't be afraid, I'm not angry—just curious."

"Hide and seek."

"The children's game?" inquired the casino proprietor.

"Not exactly. People would hide things, and I'd tell them where they were hidden. Sometimes people would lose things, and I would tell them where to find them."

"Up to the family quarters, now," ordered Momma Tereza.

Once Flynn, his mother, Nadia, and the opossum reached the family quarters, Momma Tereza demanded a full explanation. After hearing about Natsu-now-Nadia's creation, upbringing, escape with singing opossum Hoshi-now-Honey, Momma clapped her hands. "You are the real thing! You can probably do more than tea leaves and recovering lost items."

Then, Momma Tereza grimaced. "We will have to arrange for the assassin to kill you, or there will be no peace."

"What!" gasped Nadia.

Honey started to wail.

"Hush," said Flynn as he stroked the girl's hair.

His mother grabbed the opossum and began to calm the creature. "We've got to make it look like the assassin fulfilled their contract and murdered you. But how?"

"Someone mention assassins?" Jaffee strode into the room.

"We need to make them think they've eliminated their target, so they'll fly back to Gulzar sure of their success and reward," said Momma. "First, we need two bodies." She scrutinized Nadia. "Petite female with dark hair." The woman glanced down at Honey. "And a dead gray opossum."

"I'll handle the bodies," said Jaffee. He made an obscene gesture at Flynn, bowed to Momma Tereza and Nadia, turned, and walked out the door.

"They will do blood-work on the body to confirm it's their Gen-Engs." Flynn picked up his mother's business directory. "Do you still have a doctor on staff?"

"Of course. I have several. The question is, which one owes me the biggest debt and which one can I force to keep a secret." Momma Tereza handed Honey to Nadia. "Don't worry about a thing. I know who we'll use. You two wait here."

After his mother left the room, Flynn sat next to Nadia on the sofa. He rubbed her creamy jaw, ran his fingertips down her neck and collarbone. Nadia turned and pressed her body against his. Their kiss deepened as he slid his hand down to her waist. Then, Honey warbled.

"Jeeze, I'm going to go deaf if she does that in my ear again," Flynn complained.

"Good thing, though," whispered Nadia. "I hear your mother coming down the hall, and I don't want her to think I'm a hussy."

Flynn threw back his head and laughed. "A hussy? I don't think I've ever heard that word used in conversation before." He laughed again, then kissed Nadia on her cheek.

"Ah, young love." Momma Tereza was back, accompanied by a sallow-skinned man. "Nadia, roll up your sleeve. Flynn, get a firm hold on Honey."

The doctor produced two needles, two plexi-vials, a couple of antiseptic swab packets, some gauze pads, and surgical tape. Without speaking, he rubbed Honey's right foreleg with an alcohol swab, jabbed it with a needle, withdrew a vial of blood, and taped a gauze pad firmly over the puncture wound. He marked the vial with an *M*. Still not talking, he repeated the procedure, taking a vial's worth of Nadia's blood from her arm.

Flynn noticed when the doctor pressed the gauze pad on the puncture mark on Nadia's arm, his hands trembled. Whatever his drug of choice, he suspected Momma had promised him several months' supply for his services.

"Good work, Doctor. You may go back to your gaming table," said Momma Tereza. After the man exited the family quarters, the casino owner turned to Nadia. "Now, to arrange your death."

"Done," boasted Jaffee as he stuck his head in the doorway. "Come on, you two, and bring the squawking, rat-tailed beast. Momma, you better go down onto the floor where everyone can see you."

"Ah, Jaffee," crooned Momma Tereza as she patted her step-nephew on the cheek and handed him the vials of blood. "What would I do without you?"

"Be sad and lonely." The trucker winked at his aunt, and then, led Flynn and Nadia down a stairwell towards the loading area.

"Is the woman from The Wayfarer here yet?" Flynn asked.

"Yup," responded Jaffee. "I've confirmed through my sources that she is in The Canyons and on her way to the subterranean freight train platforms."

"Freight train platforms?"

"She thinks she can sneak up into The Third Eye undetected from there with a beer delivery from the Gitano Brewery."

"Not bad," said Flynn. "So how we playing this once we meet up with the assassin?"

"Don't worry, Cuz. Follow my lead." Jaffee produced a set of keys and unlocked a steel door. "We'll use this elevator to go down to the freight train platforms. She should be showing up any minute."

"Will you kill her?" There were creases between Nadia's eyebrows. "There's got to be another option."

"We could offer her a bribe—she might take it," suggested Flynn. "But if she declines…"

"There would still be loose ends if we let her leave The Canyons," warned Jaffee. "Loose ends are trouble waiting to happen."

The elevator doors opened onto a poorly lit subway. A large tunnel rat waddled across the tracks to their left, paused, glanced back in their direction, and then, disappeared between two pieces of wood. There were barrels, boxes, and crates stacked helter-skelter along dozens of concrete piers.

"Jaffee?" a female voice called from the other side of a tower of Gitano Beer boxes.

"Over here, Truda," the trucker put a finger to his lips and drew a gun out from his waistband with the other hand. "Platform Six," he called out.

"Whew, nasty place," said the female assassin as she stepped out from behind a support column. "Brought them both and the animal, I see."

"Yup. As we discussed, Truda. Go collect your DNA specimens and retinal scans. Once you have confirmed their identities, we can finish things up."

As assassin Truda scanned first the opossum's eyes, then the girl's, Flynn tried to signal his cousin. Jaffee shook his head side-to-side. Next, Truda pricked Honey and Nadia with tiny needles that protruded from the top of her communicator.

"Info sent to Gulzar. We should hear back from the Ziya Research Facility in a few minutes." The woman smiled and blew Jaffee a kiss. "This is it, lover. By tomorrow night, we will be off this planet, enjoying the rest of our lives as rich, retired government employees."

"What?" Flynn turned to his cousin. "Jaffee, what is going on?"

"Sorry, Cuz," said the big man. "I wasn't ever gonna inherit The Third Eye or anything else with you out there roaming Marawa. Gotta make your own fortune sometimes." Jaffee tipped his head towards Truda. "Met this lady a few years back, and together, we've been eliminating Gen-Engs for the Gulzar politicians. Our account is so full of credits, we'll never spend them all."

"And Natsu is our final target," Truda said, then licked her lips. "You made it tougher on us, fleeing cross-country. But in the end, you're going to die like all the lab rats before you."

"But not the scientists, you didn't kill the luminous scientist Gen-Engs with dim light vision," said Nadia-who-used-to-be-Natsu.

"Sorry, sweetheart," said Jaffee. "When the Gulzar higher-ups decided to delete all records of the Ziya Luminescent Gen-Eng Experiments, everyone had to be eliminated—scientist or not."

"Clean slate," added Truda, as she ran her fingers through her short, yellow hair. She studied her communicator. "They're taking too long."

"Patience, love," said Jaffee in a calm voice.

"Momma Tereza will have you killed for this," promised Flynn.

"She has gotta find me first."

"She'll track you through your credit record, flight schedule, something. You're bound to leave a trail."

"I don't think so, Flynn. Everything is in joint accounts using Truda's name."

"What's to prevent her from murdering you and keeping it all?" Flynn studied the blond, wondered where she hid the blowpipe and darts. In her jacket, he supposed. He took a small step towards Truda.

"Hold it right there, Cuz." Jaffee raised his gun slightly. "By the way, there's a price on your head, too."

"Yeah. I thought there might be," replied Flynn. "But Momma will pay you ten times the amount not to kill me."

"Don't matter," said Jaffee with a wave of the gun. "Driver who wants your route paid me this morning."

"And you took the job?"

Jaffee shrugged his shoulders. "I already plan to leave Marawa, so extra credits for an easy hit are always nice." He looked over at his partner and asked, "Darling, have we heard from Gulzar?"

"Yeah," answered Truda. She punched a final response into the communicator and sent a message. "The identity of our targets is confirmed, the last payment of credits for a job well done has been deposited in our account." The assassin snapped the device closed, tossed it on the tracks. "And they don't need to inspect the bodies." Truda lifted her gun and pointed it at Flynn.

"In answer to your question, Flynn, nothing prevents Truda from killing me and keeping all the credits—nothing except love." The trucker whipped the gun barrel around, shot Truda in the forehead before she could react. "And love stinks," added Jaffee.

"Jeeze, Jaffee, you had me believing you'd turned on Momma and the rest of the Travelers." Flynn stepped towards his cousin.

"Stay back, Flynn. Sorry, but I can't leave any loose ends, and you two," he waved his gun around again, "are loose ends. If you hadn't hooked up with Nadia-Natsu there and her noisy opossum, you wouldn't have to die." The trucker sighed. "Sorry about this, Cuz. You know, I always liked you."

"Wait," said Flynn. "The Gulzar officials have already deposited the credits in Truda's account. We are dead to them. Just tie Nadia and me up. By the time we're discovered, you'll be in the air to Gulzar."

"By the time your bodies are discovered, I *will* be in the air to Gulzar."

"What about blood ties? The Code of the Travelers?"

"What about it?" Jaffee spit on the platform. "Travelers are thieves and liars—always have been. I am just carrying on a family tradition." He raised the gun up to eye level and opened his mouth to speak.

But before he could pull the trigger, Nadia screamed and tossed her hissing opossum at Jaffee. As the girl's cries echoed in the train tunnels, Flynn dropped to the platform floor and scrambled towards Truda's body. He picked up her gun, rolled onto his back, and shot his cousin in the chest.

In slow motion, Jaffee's knees buckled, and he slumped to the floor. The Gen-Eng marsupial continued to howl and bite and dig into the assassin Jaffee's head. Flynn crawled to his cousin's body and pried Honey off of Jaffee's bloody face. Clumps of flesh dangled from the opossum's teeth and claws. Crying, Nadia crept into Flynn's arms.

"It's over," he assured her. "Natsu is dead, Hoshi is dead, and the assassins are dead." Hoping his words were true, Flynn nuzzled her hair, and then, contemplated his cousin's body. "I need a favor."

"Anything, Flynn." Nadia and her pet regarded him with their strange eyes.

"Don't tell Momma about Jaffee. Let her think he died trying to save us."

"Okay," Nadia mumbled. "Okay."

Flynn lifted the girl to her feet and picked up the opossum. "Nadia and her singing opossum, Honey. It does sound like a great act for The Third Eye."

He touched her softly glowing cheek, then took her hand, and headed towards the elevator. As their footsteps echoed through the hall, Flynn prayed things hadn't changed too much since Jaffee and he had their last ill-fated adventure. He prayed it was still easy to get away with murder on Marawa Prime.

About the Author

Born in the Year of the Dragon, Vonnie Winslow Crist, BS Art-Education and MS Professional Writing, has had a life-long interest in reading, writing, art, myth, fairytales, folklore, legends, and science fiction. Her speculative writing has been nominated for Pushcart Awards and won several Writers of the Future Contest Honorable Mentions, a Maryland State Arts Council Grant, National League of American Pen Women Writing Contests, and other awards. A cloverhand who has found so many 4-leafed clovers she keeps them in jars, Vonnie believes the world around us is filled with miracles, mystery, and magic. Check her website: www.vonniewinslowcrist.com for more information about Vonnie and her writing and art.